A Bad Wind Blowing:

A Ballysea Mystery

Frances Powell

Copyright 2016 by Frances Powell

ISBN: 978-1-48357-508-7

Cover Photos By: Eric & Martine Libotte - Creces

Cover Design By: Jo Stallings

This book is dedicated to my husband, Russell, for putting up with all my eccentricities and Eric & Martine Libotte-Creces for graciously allowing the photographs of their magnificent Wolfhounds to grace the cover.

"I will give thee a dog which I got in Ireland.

He is huge of limb and for a follower equal to an able man.

Moreover, he hath a man's wit and will bark at thine enemies but never at thy friends.

He will see by each man's face whether he be ill or well disposed towards thee,

He will lay down his life for thee"

From The Saga of Nial, 970-1014

Chapter 1

A fierce spring gale blew off the Atlantic throughout the night battering the west coast Irish village Cat Murphy and her Irish Wolfhound, The O'Brien, called home. When the day dawned, a boat found floundering outside the harbor was brought to shore. None of the crew were found aboard...only their blood.

It had only been a year since Catherine Murphy and her Irish Wolfhound, The O'Brien, moved from Annapolis, Maryland to County Sligo, Ireland after her husband of 20 years betrayed her. He had chosen Christmas Eve to announce not only was he having an affair with someone young enough to be their daughter but he also wanted a quickie divorce so they could marry before their child was born. It had come as a terrible shock to Cat. She never envisioned this affair.

She was determined to not let him know how devastated this news left her. For years she wanted a child only to be told he was happy just as they were and he didn't want anyone or anything to spoil the life they had together. She bought into his lie and now she was left alone.

3

A week later, as she walked along the shore of the Chesapeake Bay she had fallen and was knocked unconscious. Regaining consciousness in the hospital she found a freckle-faced, sandy haired man sitting by her bed.

"You took a very nasty fall but the doctors say you'll be fine, just some bruising and stiffness. I found you and called 911 for the ambulance. My name is Jeff Hunter. I recently bought Cliff House right up from where you fell," explained the stranger.

"Thank you Mr. Hunter. I was alone in the house so it really is lucky you happened to come by. I suppose it could have been much worse."

"It certainly could have been. Actually, I wasn't even on the beach this morning. If it hadn't been for your big dog coming bounding out of nowhere and scaring me half to death then you would probably still be lying there or worse yet floating in the Bay."

Cat looked at him in confusion as he continued the story of her rescue.

"I tried shooing him away but he was so persistent. He kept running up to me and barking and then running toward the beach and looking back at me. Anyway, I finally got the idea he wanted me to follow him. When I did, I found you there. He has lying beside you with his big head across you. He's amazing. That's some dog you have there," said a beaming Mr. Hunter.

"Mr. Hunter, what dog are you talking about? I don't own a dog."

That day marked the beginning of the friendship between Cat Murphy and Jeff Hunter and after a month of trying to locate the owner of the stray Irish Wolfhound, they named him The O'Brien after their favorite pub. It was after one of their evenings out when they returned to Jeff's house to find a letter from a Dublin solicitor advising him he had inherited his aunt's house in Ballysea, a small fishing village on the west coast of Ireland.

"Now, what am I going to do with another house and one in Ireland to boot? I've only been to Ballysea once as a teenager with my mother when

Uncle Patrick passed away," confided Jeff as he leaned forward to light Cat's after dinner cigarette,

"I'm so sorry to hear of your aunt's passing but what wouldn't I give for such a letter. What could be more perfect?" said Cat with a sigh.

"Perfect? Do you really mean you would up and move to Ireland, just like that?"

"It would be a the perfect time to do it. I could finally finish my book before my publisher disowns me and my lease is nearly up," mused Cat.

"And you would go there all alone not knowing anything about the place and not knowing anyone? And that's even if you would be allowed to immigrate," asked Jeff.

"Oh, there wouldn't be a problem with immigration. Since both my grandparents were born and raised in Sligo I could apply for citizenship under the Grandparent Clause. And as for me being alone," replied Cat, as she smiled and reached down to pat the big dog lying at her feet, "The O'Brien can come with me. All he needs is his shots and a pet passport."

Talking into the early hours of the morning, Jeff described the small harbor side village Cat would be calling her new home.

"It reminds me a bit of Annapolis, except not so commercial," said Jeff as he chuckled and continued. "Well, maybe I should say not commercial at all. Since the EU put all the fishing restrictions in place there isn't a lot happening at the harbor. As I recall, most of the town's people depend on the big house for their livelihood. The last time I was there, the whole town consisted of a couple of shops which met the everyday needs of the town people, but for anything else you'd need to go into Sligo."

"Big house?" asked Cat.

"Yeah, there is a manor house which sits outside town. It's apparently been in the same family for generations and with them owning over a hundred acres they employ half of the village. Those who don't work there depend on trade from the manor to keep their businesses afloat."

Cat and The O'Brien moved to Ballysea that very Spring seeking peace and quiet; however, peace and quiet was far from what they found in the sleepy village that first year. With The O'Brien's habit of digging up skeletons and two attempts on her life, Cat was hoping the coming of this new Spring would finally bring with it the peace and quiet she needed to finish researching her latest novel.

After a damp and cold winter, Spring had arrived again in Ballysea. Cat's hard work planting new bulbs in her cottage garden the previous Autumn was rewarded by daffodils and tulips springing forth in brilliant yellow, red and oranges hues. Stepping outside the front door of her whitewashed cottage on the first bright day in weeks, Cat spied her friend and neighbor, Maureen, already on her knees and busy at work weeding her own front garden. Cat and Maureen had become close friends during the early days of Cat's arrival when the red headed, freckle-faced Maureen had shown up on her doorstep with freshly baked warm scones. The visits quickly turned into a daily ritual with the exchange of coffee and a cigarette for Maureen's fresh baked goods.

Cat had long thought the village should revive the weekly market and encourage the town's people with particular skills, such as Maureen's, to sell their wares there. The idea was one she planned on presenting to Maureen over their morning coffee but first it was time for The O'Brien to have his morning ramble down the beach. Just like his mistress, The O'Brien had his strict schedule to keep. It had become his singular morning mission to keep the sandy beach free of gulls and he delighted in chasing them anytime given the opportunity. Today would be no exception.

Once the coffee was set to brew, Cat called back to the still snoozing O'Brien, "Come on O'Brien, walkies." The O'Brien was a little slow getting to his feet this morning due to a restless night during which a gale howled around the little cottage. With no buffer between the sea and her small house, except for the narrow lane, Cat's cottage took the full brunt of the wind. For as big and fearless as he was, The O'Brien did not like the wind.

As the giant of a dog slowly ambled over to Cat's side she stooped down and wrapping her arms around him said, "I know big fellow, I didn't like that wind last night either."

The O'Brien preferred his own dog bed to any of the furniture in the house so it surprised Cat when she felt her bed shake as he gently climbed in beside her and snuggled up as close as he could. Sometime during the night she was roughly shaken awake as he jumped from the bed and ran down the stairs. He continued to howl at the door until Cat staggering downstairs from bed still half asleep eventually managed to coax him back upstairs to bed.

Walking down her front walk and across the narrow lane, Cat called to Maureen, "We'll be back in a few minutes. The coffee's brewing."

Finished her weeding, Maureen scrambled to her feet and wiping the dirt from her hands waved back and hollered, "Coffee sounds great. I made some wild strawberry jam for our scones this morning so I'll bring that along."

Smiling back, Cat continued walking down towards the beach. As The O'Brien went off patrolling the perimeter of the beach, Cat sat on the large flat rock at the bottom of the rock face which trailed down from the cliff to the sea. Finally finished his romp, The O'Brien returned to Cat and promptly shook himself in front of her. Water and sand flying everywhere, Cat exclaimed, "Well, thanks a lot. No treat for you this morning. You could have done that over there," she said pointing in the direction of the far end of the beach nearest the harbor. It was only then that she noticed a flurry of activity at the normally sleepy harbor.

As she pointed, she noticed the figure of a tall man walking along the small stretch of beach in her direction. As he drew nearer, she recognized Edward Granville, one of the owners of the manor which sat outside of Ballysea. A ruggedly handsome man with a thick black hair and warm brown eyes, Edward and Cat had become friends over the last year when she and Jeff had taken it upon themselves to delve into the mystery surrounding the disappearance of Edward's young heiress wife. Their snooping around had almost cost Cat her very life. Since that time Edward made a habit of stopping by Cat's cottage for a coffee and a chat on weekends when he was in town. During the week, he and his younger brother Ryan kept extremely busy sharing the responsibility of raising Edward's wife's daughter Marian, and managing the manor and its hundred acres.

"Good Morning Cat and how's my friend O'Brien this morning?" asked Edward as he reached down and patted the wet dog's back.

Laughing, Cat replied, "He's managed to get himself soaked today. Seems there was one stubborn gull that just refused to stay off The O'Brien's own personal beach. We're going up to meet Maureen for coffee. Have you got time to stop in for a visit?"

Giving her a rakish grin, Edward gazed down into the blue eyes of the petite blond and replied, "Now, when wouldn't I have time for the two best looking women within a hundred miles, not to mention the most handsome hound in all of Ireland?"

Slipping her arm through Edward's offered arm, the friends made the short walk up to Cat's cottage to find Maureen had already set the table with three mugs and spoons.

"Morning Edward, I saw you coming and I thought you might like some coffee," said Maureen as she filled the coffee mugs.

Dropping his 6'2" frame into the nearest chair, Edward replied, "Coffee and plenty of it. It's been a long night."

Suddenly concerned Cat asked, "Is everything alright up at the manor? Marian isn't ill is she?"

"No, everyone and everything at the manor is fine but I was called out in the middle of that gale last night for a boat in distress. I thought maybe one of you may have heard something."

Both women looked at each other and shook their heads. Then suddenly, Cat looked over at The O'Brien and exclaimed, "Is that what you were trying to tell me big fellow?"

Raising his eyebrow, Edward looked from Cat to The O'Brien and asked, "What happened?"

Cat explained about The O'Brien's fear of the wind and that she thought the terrible gales had upset him and caused the howling.

"Do you remember what time that was?" asked Edward.

"No, I'm sorry. I was half asleep and I didn't look at the clock. I only wanted to get him calmed down. He was extremely agitated. Why? What's happened Edward?"

"There was a boat in trouble right outside the harbor last night. By the time we were able to get to it there was no one on board."

Crossing herself, Maureen asked, "Do you think they fell overboard and drowned?"

"It doesn't look like it. The cabin was really messed up like there had been some type of fight and then there was the blood. I've never seen so much blood before," replied Edward as he grimaced and finished the last of his coffee before standing to leave.

With one more pat to The O'Brien's head, Edward walked to the door and said, "Thanks for the coffee ladies. If I hear anymore, I'll let you know. If you see anything out of the ordinary give me a call and I'll be right over."

Closing the door behind him, Cat plopped down at the old farmhouse table, lit a cigarette and passing one to Maureen said, "I thought nothing ever happened in this village. Well, so much for this being a peaceful spring. Here we go again."

Chapter 2

As the sun was just coming up on another misty Spring morning, Cat was already on her second cup of coffee and peering out her door at the scene playing out at the harbor below. The abandoned boat had finally been brought up on shore and was cordoned off by the Garda as they performed their criminal investigation. Teams of forensic investigators could be seen boarding the boat and carrying off what appeared to be evidence and undoubtedly samples of the blood Edward had mentioned.

As Cat stood watching from her door, The O'Brien rose from his bed near the coal fire Cat had lit to take off the damp early morning chill and rambled over and slipped his big head under her hand.

"What's up big guy? Are you waiting for your run on the beach?" asked Cat as she stroked the big dog's head.

Pulling her mackintosh from the row of brightly painted pegs beside the front door, Cat slipped into her coat and the two housemates headed across the lane to the beach below.

Settling herself once more on the large flat rock, Cat continued to watch the activities going on at the harbor while The O' Brien charged back and forth chasing the gulls.

Suddenly a voice from behind her asked, "Come here often, gorgeous?"

Recognizing the soft seductive voice of Ryan Granville, the younger of the Granville brothers, Cat replied smiling, "Good Morning Ryan. How are things up at the manor?"

"Things are fine but about to get very busy. It's close to spring lambing time so Edward and I are going to be kept very busy. I stopped by today to see if you wanted to come see the lambing."

"I'd love to," replied Cat thinking, 'Might make good research for a future book.'

"Great. Be sure to bring The O'Brien with you. Marian has been asking for him and would love to see him and you too of course," replied Ryan.

Calling The O'Brien, Cat said, "We're just going up to meet Maureen for coffee and scones. Can I tempt you?"

17

Throwing his head back and laughing, "That's a loaded question. But I must confess you could tempt me even without the offer of coffee and scones."

"Oh, go on with you! Your Irish is showing, " replied Cat playfully poking him in his ribs.

As they walked back to the cottage Cat asked, "So anymore news about the crew missing from the boat?"

"Not as far as I know, but Edward is still down there this morning and if I'm not sadly mistaken he'll be stopping at your place before he leaves the village," said Ryan winking.

"And what exactly is that wink supposed to mean?"asked Cat.

"Oh come on, you seriously don't realize my big brother is crazy about you? And quite frankly, if I hadn't taken an oath not to constantly try to best my brother, I would give him a run for his money," replied Ryan deliberately winking at Cat again until she burst out laughing as they entered the cottage and settled themselves at the table.

The sudden thumping of O'Brien's tail followed by a gentle knock at Cat's door announced the arrival of Maureen.

"Come in, the door's open," yelled Cat as she started to set the table for coffee and scones.

"Morning Cat. Morning Ryan. Better set the table for four. I just saw Edward heading up the lane in this direction," said Maureen as she deposited the freshly baked scones on the table and pulled a chair out and sat down opposite Ryan. "And good morning to you too O'Brien," she continued as the big dog ambled over to the table and began to root around in the pocket of her apron with his nose.

"You can't fool him, Maureen. He could smell that treat in your pocket from across the lane," said a smiling Cat.

The sudden knock on the door announcing Edward's arrival had all three of them shouting, "Come in!"

"Looks like the gang's all here," said Edward smiling as he strode into the kitchen and taking off his leather jacket dropped into the nearest available chair.

As Cat poured everyone their coffee, she asked, "Any news on the boat and its missing crew?"

"Not a lot really. The Garda know the boat and its crew previously berthed in Sligo and there were at least two men on board but there may have been more."

"How do they know that?" asked Ryan.

"One of the bartenders at a pub close to the harbor gave a description of them. Apparently, he was walking to work past the harbor when they stopped him and asked directions to a pub close to the harbor. He remembered the name of the vessel they got off, the Lady Gray."

Passing around the scones, Maureen asked, "Now what?"

"Looks like we'll just have to wait for the Garda to finish their investigation. I guess they'll need to find the bodies first. They're checking points south of here to see if the bodies wash ashore."

Finishing his coffee, Edward grabbed his brother by the arm and laughed," We best be getting back to the manor. There are a lot of ladies up there depending on us."

As soon as the two brothers closed the cottage door behind them, Maureen turned to Cat asking, "Ladies? What ladies?"

"The four-legged kind. Apparently, lambing has started," explained Cat with a smile.

Chapter 3

The following morning over coffee, Maureen offered to drop Cat off at the manor on her way to do some shopping in Sligo.

As they made the short drive to the manor, Maureen said, "I'm really curious about that boat and what happened on it so I might ask around while I'm in town and see what gossip I can pick up."

"Good idea," replied Cat. "I'll ask Edward if he has any news too. I also want to ask him for his support in starting up the weekly market in town again."

"That's a great idea. I for one would love having the market back. Not only would it be a good place for people to sell their wares but it would build community spirit and create an atmosphere where neighbors can become better acquainted."

Arriving at the manor, Maureen parked in front and let Cat and The O'Brien out just as Edward exited the kitchen door.

"Hey ladies! You here for the lambing, Cat? Ryan mentioned you might drop by."

Hanging out the car window, Maureen waved and yelled, "I'll be back around 4 to pick you up."

"Perfect. Thanks for the lift! Drive carefully," called Cat.

"I take it you haven't witnessed lambing before," said Edward as he and Cat walked across the drive to the barn.

"No, I'm afraid I've lived in towns my whole life and the closest I've been to sheep is seeing them grazing in the fields around here."

"Well, sheep are seasonal breeders, unlike a lot of other animals, and they mate in the fall and lamb in the spring months when it's warmer and there is a good supply of grass. We normally round them up and bring them into the field closest to the barn so we can keep an eye on them. Most of the time, they can manage the birthing on their own but if they need us then one of us will be there. Ryan and I take it in shifts, so they're never left alone."

"So, how do you know when they are about to deliver?" asked Cat as they strolled to the fenced in paddock.

Laughing Edward replied, "Ewes are a lot like most other ladies. They like their privacy. When labor starts they'll wander away from the herd to find a quiet spot to lamb. You can usually set your clock by that and within an hour or so they go into labor."

"So how come you and Ryan have to stand watch over them day and night?"

"Well, lambs are normally born head first with their front feet tucked up under their chin but like with human babies they can be breach and when that happens it's all hands on deck or in this case in the ewe. We need to help turn the lamb so it can be born. Once the lamb is born the mother takes over clearing the mucus membrane and we keep watch until the second lamb arrives. It's usually about a fifteen minute ordeal for both lambs to be delivered but when you have over a hundred ewes it can be quite exhausting."

"I don't know how you two manage all this on your own," replied Cat in awe.

Laughing out loud Edward continued, "And exactly why do you think we invited you here today?"

"You are kidding!" exclaimed Cat as she began backing away from the fence.

"Well, partially. You see sometimes for one reason or another the mother will reject the lamb or she might just not have enough milk to feed both of them and that's where you come in. You can help take care of the orphans, as we call them, and feed them. We keep a supply of bottles on hand. Think you can handle the feeding if the occasion arises today?"

Breathing a sigh of relief she wouldn't be assisting in the actual deliveries Cat smiled and said, "I'd be delighted. I've always loved feeding babies and this can't be much different."

"Not much different at all. When and if the situation arises, I'll show you how to hold the lamb and give it the bottle. In the meantime, I have a thermos of hot tea and some biscuits in the barn.

25

We might as well relax and chat until we're needed."

Dropping down on the bales of hay he'd set up to serve as their seats, the two began talking about the police investigation.

"Have you had any more news yet on the victims?" asked Cat between bites of her biscuit.

"Nothing, other than what I told you the other day. It's really quite a mystery at this point but one thing I can tell you is, whoever that blood belonged to didn't die quickly," continued Edward.

"How do you know ?" asked Cat.

"Quite simply, once you are dead, your heart stops pumping blood through the body. The amount of blood I saw clearly indicated someone had been bleeding a long time before they died and disappeared off the boat."

"And no one has been reported missing?"

"It's early days yet and if the people on board were expected to be gone on their sailing trip for an extended period then perhaps their families or friends have no idea there's a problem," explained Edward.

"Well, surely the Garda have checked the boat registration and have an address for the owner."

"That's what they were trying to track down last I heard but I guess we'll just have to wait until we hear something," replied Edward shrugging.

Cat and Edward were just finishing their tea when a sleepy eyed Ryan came wandering into the barn.

"Afternoon all," said the yawning Ryan.

"You're up early. I wasn't expecting you to take over your shift for at least another two hours," noted Edward after glancing at his watch.

"Yeah I know. Marian was practicing the piano downstairs and I do believe that she really dislikes Chopin."

Smiling Cat asked, "Why do you say that?"

"Because she sure is murdering him and the language...oh my. I don't mind telling you that she didn't learn those words from me," replied Ryan as he pointed his finger in his brother's direction.

"It's bloody this and bloody that," continued Ryan.

Cat couldn't help but laugh when she recalled her first meeting with Ryan when he had used those exact words after he nearly collided with Maureen's stalled car the previous Spring. "Sounds like the kettle calling the pot black," said Cat.

Laughing and feigning shock Ryan replied, "I don't know what you mean!"

Cat passed a cup of tea to Ryan and sat back and watched the two brother's congenial exchange and thought how much their relationship had changed since last year. All the animosity had been replaced by genuine brotherly love and a true bonding since the death of their deranged murderous father. It was if a dark cloud had been lifted from the manor and all those that lived there.

As the three sat comfortably talking, they were joined by Garda Burke who had just arrived from the harbor. Mike Burke was Ballysea's local Garda and although he worked out of the constabulary in Sligo, he made his home in Ballysea and had actually grown up in one of the workman's' crofts on the manor. Hearing the car pull up in the drive, Ryan went to the door of the barn and called, "We're in here Mike."

Entering the barn, Garda Burke pulled up a bale of hay and joined the group of friends. Having been a playmate to Ryan and Edward when youngsters they had remained close friends.

"Any more news, Mike?" asked Edward.

"Yes and No. We found out the boat is registered to a woman named Maeve Butler at 3 Park Place in Dublin. We contacted the Dublin Garda Síochána and they informed us there's no such address in Dublin. They also ran her name through their files and they can't find any record of the woman. So until we find some remains and can identify them, we're struggling," replied Mike shrugging his shoulders.

"How very strange," replied Cat.

"So, where do you go from here?" asked Edward.

"The boys are back in Sligo hoping to talk to someone at the pub who may have talked to the missing men or even overheard any of their conversations. I'm heading up that way myself. The wife wants me to stop in at the bakery and pick up a cake for her mother's birthday. Shame we don't still have a bakery here in Ballysea."

"Oh, that reminds me Edward, Maureen and I were talking about trying to revive the town market and we are hoping to count on your support. It's a shame for people to need to make the drive back and forth to Sligo to pick up things which could very well be made available here in the village at least once or twice a week," said Cat.

Before Edward could answer, Mike replied, "I would sure welcome it. It seems like I'm always running back and forth to pick up things my wife can't get in the village and after working in Sligo most of the day, I really just want to get back home to Ballysea and enjoy some peace and quiet."

"Well, I don't know how peaceful our little village has been the last year but compared to the cities where you have a different crime every other night then I guess it is a relief to get home," replied Ryan thoughtfully.

Edward thought for a minute and replied, "If you think you can get enough of the locals interested in starting up the market again then of course you'll have our full support. Soon as the lambing is over and things slow down, I'll be more than glad to furnish any lumber you need from our forests and the men to build new stalls."

"And you can count on me to get the word out around town," replied Garda Burke.

"I'll mention it to Mrs. O'Malley and I'm sure she'll be interested. Did you know she keeps chickens here?" asked Ryan.

"No, I didn't. That is something I've always fancied doing. Do you think she might have enough extra eggs to sell at the market?" asked Cat.

Both brothers looked at each other and burst out laughing, "She has so many we end up eating eggs of one sort or another for almost every meal, so you'd be doing us a huge favor!" replied Edward.

As the day wore on, a number of ewes had delivered. Only one new mother needed help feeding one of her lambs. After being shown by Edward how to hold the lamb and present the bottle Cat was well into feeding the little orphan when the sound of a car in the gravel drive announced Maureen's return from Sligo. Bounding into the barn, she looked over at Cat feeding the lamb and beamed, "Look at you! You're a natural. You would think you were raised on a sheep farm."

"Edward showed me how and I must say I am really enjoying it," beamed a glowing Cat.

"And what does our The O'Brien think of all this?" asked Maureen her eyes searching the dimly lit barn for The O'Brien.

"I think he's more interested in Ryan's sheep dog at the moment," said Cat as she smiled and pointed to the one sunny spot in the barn where both dogs lay curled up together peacefully sleeping.

"Well, looks like they've become fast friends," replied Maureen smiling at the sight.

"Learn anything interesting in town?" asked Cat.

"I stopped in at the pub where those two men ate and talked to the waitress. She told me they were flashing around a lot of cash...big bills. And while she was serving them their food, she overheard them talking about their boss. She got the impression their boss was a woman and they didn't trust her."

"Did she say anything else, Maureen?" asked Mike.

"No, but as I was leaving some of your fellow officers were coming in. I'm sure if she or anyone else remembers anything they'll be glad to tell the officers."

"Thanks for the information Maureen. I appreciate it. Sometimes a woman feels more comfortable talking to another woman than talking to us," replied Mike gratefully.

"No problem, but I'm going to have to steal Cat away from you guys. I need to get home and get dinner on for the family," replied Maureen.

Calling The O'Brien to her side, Cat and Maureen waved goodbye to the three men and climbed into Maureen's vintage CSV and headed home to Ballysea

Chapter 4

Early the next morning as Cat was stumbling around her kitchen trying to get the ancient stove to heat up so she could put the kettle on there was a soft knock at the door. Yelling, "Wait a minute," she hurried to the door with The O'Brien at her side. Standing outside was Garda Mike Burke and the look on his face could only be described as grim.

"Come on in Mike and have a seat. I've finally managed to get the kettle on. Silly old stove's been acting up the last couple of days. I suppose I'm going to need to get someone in to look at it."

"My mam has one just like it and if you want I can take a look at it for you tomorrow on my day off, if that's not too late for you."

"That would be great Mike. I'd appreciate it. So what brings you here so early and why are you looking so pale. You're not ill are you?" asked Cat as she slid a mug of coffee over in front of the young officer.

"No I'm not sick, but we did have something of a break early this morning in the case of those two men missing from the boat and I don't mind telling you, it wasn't a pleasant sight," replied Mike.

"Can you talk about it?" asked Cat as she slid into a chair opposite the young Garda.

"Yes. I'm sure it'll be all over the village soon enough. Quite a crowd was already starting to gather around the scene. We found a body."

Pouring warm milk into her coffee Cat replied, "Well, that's good, isn't it? At least now you can identify one of them and maybe find out what happened on that boat."

"Well, we think we may have an idea of what happened on the boat but we're going to have a much harder job identifying him," grimaced Mike.

"Oh, I guess he'd been in the water too long, huh?" responded Cat making a face as she stirred her coffee.

Turning very white, Mike said, "Well that too and the fact he was missing his hands, feet and head isn't going to help."

Dropping her spoon, Cat exclaimed, "How horrible. No wonder you've gone all ashen!"

"That's not even the worse of it Cat. He'd been gutted. Looks like he was sliced right open and his innards removed."

"Why in the world would someone do that to another human being?" asked Cat.

"Drug smugglers, we're guessing. He had probably ingested the drugs and someone was in a hurry to get them out. So far only one body has washed up so we aren't sure if the other man is the perpetrator or if the woman they talked about at the pub in Sligo is involved. The forensics team is down there and getting ready to take what's left of the poor devil to the morgue for a DNA sample. With any luck he may be in our database then we can identity him and maybe track down his associates."

"If Edward's theory about the amount of blood found on the boat is right then the poor soul must have been alive when at least one or more of those horrible things was done to him," said Cat as she shuddered.

37

"Sadly, it would appear that way."

A sudden thumping of The O'Brien's tail and a soft knock at the door announced the arrival of Maureen.

"Come on in, Maureen," yelled Cat as she poured another cup of coffee.

Taking one look at Mike, Maureen asked, "Are you alright Mike?"

"Yes, I'm fine. I was going off shift and just stopped in to tell Cat a body has been found. I need to be getting home but she can fill you in on the details."

"Do you want a bacon butty before you leave? I have extras."

"No thanks. I think I've lost my appetite," replied Mike and waving goodbye he was out the door. Maureen sat quietly drinking her coffee and feeding bacon to The O'Brien while Cat filled her in on all the details. When Cat finished talking, Maureen saw the look on her friend's face and thought, 'Oh no, here we go again. I have a feeling somehow this spells more danger for Cat and The O'Brien.'

Chapter 5

The rest of the day passed quickly for Cat as she took advantage of the bright day to work in her small cottage garden. Cat had never seen weeds grow as quickly as they did here in Ireland but put it down to the amount of rain they seemed to get. As she weeded she thought, 'Guess weeds are the price we pay for these beautiful emerald green fields.' Cat loved walking with The O'Brien in the fields just beyond her cottage. Being the last cottage on the lane she was blessed with not only magnificent sea views directly across the lane but also views of beautiful open fields leading up to the rock faced cliff beyond. Just recently, Cat had invested in a digital camera to take photographs on her walks and had managed to get quite a few that she hoped would make good covers for her novels. She laughed out loud when she thought about the hilarious selfies that she and Maureen had taken at her kitchen table stuffing their faces with the scones that Jeff loved, and even harder when she thought about the immediate responses from Jeff of the emailed photos.

"I didn't know that weeding could elicit those types of responses. Frankly, I've never heard anyone on their knees laughing as they weeded," came the rich baritone voice of Edward from behind her back.

Whipping her head around, she looked over at the still snoozing O'Brien and putting her hands on her hips scolded, "Fine watch dog you are. You could have at least warned me someone was here before I made a complete fool of myself. And good morning to you too, Edward. You have time for a coffee or tea? I'd like to talk to you about the plans for the market."

The only response from O'Brien, as he dozed in the warm Spring sun, was one slight wag of his tail before closing his eyes and drifting back to sleep.

Reaching a hand down, Edward easily lifted Cat to her feet and replied, "I was hoping you'd ask."

Pulling off her weeding gloves and throwing them into her rusty old weeding bucket by the front door she patted The O'Brien's sleeping head and said, "Sorry old fellow, you're going to have to give up your warm spot. We need to get in the house."

The O'Brien groaned and begrudgingly got slowly to his feet and stood patiently waiting to follow Edward and Cat inside. Once inside Cat put the kettle on and setting the table for two asked, "Tea or coffee?"

"I think tea. I've already had a couple of cups of coffee with Mike Burke down in the village. Oh and by the way, he said he'd be up soon to have a look at your stove."

"Great, thanks. Did he tell you about the body they found?" asked Cat as she poured hot water into the tea pot to warm it before setting the tea to brew.

"Yeah, pretty nasty scene. Mike said he had nightmares all night about what the poor devil must have gone through before he finally died. He said that the preliminary blood tests were in this morning and it appears all the blood belonged to one victim so it could be that the other man committed the murder or if he was killed too then his body wasn't bludgeoned."

"Have the DNA test results come back yet?" asked Cat as she poured the now steeped tea.

42

"No. I asked Mike about that too and he said they had to be sent to the lab and it can take at least 60 hours for the tests to run and that's if they don't have a huge backlog. So it looks like it may be a couple more days before we can realistically expect to hear any more news on his possible identity and that's even if he's in the database."

"So, if he hasn't been in trouble with the law before then he won't be in the database?"

"That's the impression I got from Mike," replied Edward as he sipped his tea.

Putting her cup down, Cat asked, "How's the lambing going? Almost finished?"

Clearing his voice and trying to sound stern Edward replied, "It's going fine. Marian has taken over your position of lamb feeding since you've been reneging on your duties."

"Aww...I'm sorry. Is Marian enjoying it?"

"Actually, she's loving every moment of it. There is one little black orphan lamb who has taken to her and follows her everywhere. I went into the library the other day and found the two of them curled up

43

asleep in front of the fire. I had to explain to her that sheep don't belong in the house and she needed to get the wee little thing out before Mrs. O'Malley caught sight of it and threatened to serve him for Sunday dinner."

Ever conscious of the sensitivity of the motherless child, Cat responded, " She wouldn't say such a thing in front of Marian would she? The poor child would be devastated."

"Good god. No. Marian runs that house despite what Mrs. O'Malley would like everyone to believe and she absolutely dotes on the child. Since her brood have all grown up and moved away she enjoys playing the grandmother role with Marian. As a matter of fact, I haven't had a decent lamb dinner since Marian was old enough to start giving orders," said a laughing Edward.

"So, once lambing is done, can we still count on you for some timber and men to help build the stalls?"

"Absolutely, we already have some timber drying and a number of the men have already volunteered their services. I've also been speaking to some of the workers who live at the manor and I found there are a number of them interested in having a stall either for themselves or for their wives. Have you ever met Big Mac?"

Pushing a stray lock of hair from her forehead and looking toward the ceiling Cat shook her head slowly and replied, "I don't think so."

"Well, apparently his wife knits beautiful sweaters and sells them at other markets around the county so she would be very happy to have a stall closer to home. Ian's wife spins wool so she might be interested if she can get Ian to keep the twins for the days that the market is on. Which brings up a good point...what days are you thinking of holding these markets?"

"I haven't talked to Maureen about it yet but I was thinking maybe Tuesday or Wednesday and Saturday of course. We still have to do the advertising plan and go around to the shops here in town to see if they want to participate. We don't want to be seen as taking business away from the locals. After we do that, we'll branch out to the neighboring towns and put up some notices and see what kind of response we get."

"Sounds like you ladies have things well in hand and with that being said, I need to get back to the manor. It's my shift to watch the ewes."

Pushing back from the table, Edward stepped over the still sleeping O'Brien and heading for the door said, "Thanks for the tea. I'll call you later."

As Cat watched Edward close the door behind him and walk down the lane towards his Land Rover she looked down at O'Brien and whispered, "Now there goes a man that would make some lucky woman a good husband."

Cat's daydreaming was quickly interrupted by the sight of Mike Burke waving to Edward as he walked up the lane towards her house with toolbox in hand. Reaching down and ruffling the wiry hair on O'Brien's head she said, "Wake up sleepy head. Looks like we're getting more company."

Mike's firm knock on the door brought The O'Brien to his feet and to the door with his tail wagging. He had grown very fond of the young Garda. Cat thought the fact that he always brought morsels of beef from his uncle's butcher shop when he visited may have accounted for at least part of it but Cat also realized that The O'Brien could tell a good man when he met one and Mike Burke was a good man. O'Brien had become friends with his uncle Jim Burke, the town butcher, the first day they arrived in Ballysea. The reserved butcher having spotted The O'Brien staring in from his front window was reminded of happier childhood days when his grandfather's hound was his favorite playmate, before the loss of his daughter to the sea and the death of his grieving wife.

Throwing the door open, Cat welcomed Mike, "Coffee or Tea Mike?"

"Tea would be fine, thanks!"

"So, do you think you can fix this ancient monstrosity or do I need to call my landlord and tell him that he needs to replace the range?" asked Cat as she passed Mike a mug of tea.

"I think I can fix it. My Mam's tends to need a bit of work every so often and I've been keeping it going for years. She doesn't want to give it up.

She says it's like an old friend. But speaking of your landlord...how is Jeff and when's he coming for another visit? I would have thought as soon as he heard about the murder in town he'd have been on the first flight over to keep an eye on you."

"Well, I haven't actually mentioned it to him or I'm sure he'd be doing just that. You know how criminal lawyers can be," said Cat laughing.

What Cat hadn't figured on was the gruesome murder had in fact made the news in the States and at that very moment Jeff was seated at his computer booking a flight to Ireland.

Chapter 6

The sound of her phone ringing later that evening interrupted Cat's internet research on the novel she had just begun. During the long winter evenings she had managed to get her last novel out to the publisher and they were now pushing her for a sequel. Lately, her days were spent planning the reopening of the town market so her evenings were spent writing.

Stepping over a snoozing O'Brien, she answered the phone, "Hello."

Smiling as she recognized Edward's voice she continued, "Hey Edward. How are you?"

On the other end of the line Edward replied, "I'm great thanks. I hope I'm not interrupting anything but I called to see if you and The O'Brien might like to join Marian and I on a walk up Benbulbin tomorrow. It's meant to be a bright day and I promised to take her as a reward for helping with the lambing. She wants to see the Alpine flowers that grow there."

"Sounds great! What time would you pick us up?"

"Would 9:00 be alright with you?"

"That would be perfect. Gives me plenty of time to give O'Brien his morning run and have a quick visit with Maureen."

"Great. We'll see you then. You might want to bring The O'Brien's lead in case we need it in Sligo," continued Edward.

"Will do. I'll see you in the morning. Goodnight." Cat smiled as she hung up the phone. She really enjoyed spending time with Edward and Marian.

Looking over at The O'Brien, Cat said, "Well my friend, if we are going to walk up a mountain in the morning we better get to bed."

Turning off the lights, Cat climbed the stairs with The O'Brien trailing behind her. Settling himself on his dog bed he let out a loud sigh and fell right back to sleep.

Undressing and slipping into her sleep shirt, Cat climbed into bed pulling the cover up to her chin. As she reached over and switched off the lamp on her bedside table, she whispered, "Night night sleepy head."

The next morning did indeed dawn bright and sunny as Edward had forecast. Cat was awake and had showered and dressed before 6:00 so that she would have enough time for O'Brien's morning run on the beach and a quick coffee with Maureen. Maureen was always up and moving around her kitchen by 6:00 so she could get her husband and children fed before she sent them off to work and school so as Cat and The O'Brien went past her house she knocked at the door.

Swinging open her door, Maureen said, "My Goodness, you are up and about even earlier than usual."

"Yes, Edward has invited The O'Brien and me to go on a hike with him and Marian up Benbulbin this morning and he's picking us up at 9:00 so I won't have long for coffee and working on the advertising for the market this morning."

"That's fine. You've been working too hard anyway. I see your lights on over there late at night. You deserve a relaxing day. I'm almost done here, so you go down the beach and I'll go get the coffee ready. At least I can give you some background on where you're going," said Maureen.

"Great. I'll see you in about 20 minutes."

The O'Brien must have somehow sensed that something out of the ordinary was happening today because after one quick sweep of the beach he was ready to return home. By the time they entered the kitchen, Maureen had already made the coffee and sat smoking a cigarette.

Hanging her jacket on the peg by the door, Cat reached for O'Brien's food bowl and filling it up and refreshing his water pulled up a chair and reached for her coffee.

"So tell me about this mountain that I'm about to climb," said Cat as she sipped her coffee and reached for a cigarette.

"You'll be going up the south side. Gortarowey is a favorite place to walk and can get very busy at times because it's suitable for all ages and abilities. The parking lot at the bottom of the trail isn't very big so It's good that you are getting an early start. The trail actually begins in a forest then opens up to provide stunning close up views of Benbulbin head. Once you reach the summit, you'll see a magnificent view over the coastal plain of north County Sligo and the ocean. So be sure to take your camera."

"Is it going to be alright for The O'Brien?"

"Oh sure. You'll see a lot of people walking with their dogs there. You might want to take his lead though; there're a lot of foxes and hares up there and if you think he'll give chase it might be safer."

Laughing Cat responded, "No worries about that. It's only sea gulls he likes to chase but I'll have his lead with me anyway."

A knock at the door announced the arrival of Edward and Marian. As soon as Cat opened the door, O'Brien immediately went to greet Marian. The way that The O'Brien was drawn to children and the obvious love he felt for them led Cat to believe before he was abandoned he had his own special child who he loved very much. Sometimes when it was time for Maureen's children to get out of school, Cat would catch The O'Brien staring at the school yard as if he was waiting for someone.

"Morning ladies," said Edward as he entered the kitchen.

"Coffee, Edward? asked Maureen.

"No thanks, Maureen. I was up at 5:00 taking care of the horses and I hate to admit it but I've already had 3 cups. I'll be on a caffeine high all day," joked Edward.

"Well, you guys go ahead and get on your way. I'll take care of these dishes and lock up after myself," said Maureen shooing her friends out the door.

"Thanks Maureen. See you later," replied Cat as she and The O'Brien climbed into the Land Rover with Edward and Marian and were on their way.

It seemed like Maureen had just waved goodbye to her friends when she heard a thumping noise at the door. Grabbing a dish cloth and wiping her soapy hands she pulled the door open and found herself staring into the red rimmed eyes of Jeff Hunter.

Grabbing Jeff in a warm embrace, Maureen exclaimed, "Cat never mentioned you were

coming. You've just missed her. She and The
O'Brien have gone on a hike up Benbulbin with
Edward and Marian."

Hugging her back, Jeff responded, "She didn't tell
you I was coming because she didn't know. Now,
let's have some coffee and then you can tell me all
about this new murder."

Chapter 7

As Maureen and Jeff sat around the kitchen table discussing the discovery of the blood drenched boat and the find of the horrifically mutilated body, Cat and Edward sat comfortably chatting as they drove through Sligo heading for Gortarowey where they would leave their car.

"You being a writer, I'm sure that you are very familiar with the works of William Butler Yeats," said Edward.

"Of course I am," replied Cat.

"Did you know that he was born in Sandymount, a coastal town outside Dublin, but spent his childhood holidays here in County Sligo?"

"No, I didn't. I don't know why but I thought he was English," replied Cat.

"Well, he was educated in England and the family moved there after a while but he never forgot County Sligo. He died in France but left instructions that after a year his remains were to be moved to County Sligo and buried near

Benbulbin. He wrote the poem *Under Ben Bulben* about the area."

"That's fascinating Edward. I had no idea."

Making a turn off the road, they soon arrived at the car park and began walking through the woods toward the open fields. Edward and Cat followed along behind Marian and The O'Brien as the child searched for a glimpse of Alpine flowers.

"Don't get too far ahead Marian," called Edward as the child scampered away ahead of them.

"Don't worry Edward. The O'Brien is keeping a very close eye on her," said Cat as she pointed to the big dog walking side by side with the young girl.

Laughing Edward replied, "Seems you have been thrown over for a younger woman."

"Wouldn't be the first time! He knows his first duty is to the child and besides he trusts that you will look after me," replied Cat smiling up into Edwards long lashed brown eyes.

Reaching down and taking Cat's hand Edward replied, "That I will."

As soon as they had reached the summit, Marian was rewarded by a patch of the Alpine flowers and she excitedly explained to Cat, "You know, they don't grow anywhere else in Ireland."

"Really? And why do you suppose that is?" asked Cat tenderly as she bent down to examine the tiny flowers.

Looking at her father she replied," Because Benbulbin is magical, right Da?"

"Yes it is sweetie. If you don't believe us Cat, look over there," replied Edward as he pointed to her left.

Cat turned her gaze away from the flowers and stood and looked to the sea and valleys below. Looking another way she could see mountains. It was as if she could see the entire landscape of Ireland from just this one spot. Taking her camera from her bag she quickly began snapping pictures of the stunning views.

After about an hour at the top, Edward called to Marian who was now stretched out on the grass with her head across O'Brien's back and looking up at the clouds, "Come on little lady. Time to start back down."

The walk down seemed a lot quicker than their trek up and as they entered the car park Marian wrinkled up her nose and said, "Wow Da, what's that terrible smell?"

Before the words were even out of her mouth, The O'Brien raced ahead of them and stood crouched and barking at the boot of a beat up looking car abandoned near the end of the car park.

When The O'Brien failed to return to Cat when called Edward walked towards the car before he suddenly turned back to Cat and said, "Cat, would you help Marian into the car and stay there with her?"

"Why? What's the matter Edward?" asked Cat after putting Marian in the back seat.

"Please just do as I ask." Leaning forward to whisper in her ear he continued, "I'm a farmer and

I can smell when something is dead. If I'm not sadly mistaken, there is something or someone dead in the boot of that car and O'Brien knows it too."

Edward pulled out his mobile phone and getting a signal placed a call to the Sligo Garda before taking O'Brien by his collar and leading him back to the Land Rover.

Calling Cat to his side he told her in hushed tones, "I've called the Garda but we'll need to wait until they arrive. It shouldn't be too long. They said they have a car in the area."

Leaning over she whispered to Edward, "Would you like me to take Marian for a walk before they get here?"

"Yes. I don't know what we're liable to find."

A few minutes later Cat said, "Marian, I'm afraid The O'Brien needs to go for a bathroom break. If I put his lead on him, do you think you're strong enough to walk him?"

"Sure Cat. Actually, I think I might have to go too so you can hold him while I go in the bathroom."

"Sounds like a good plan. The bathrooms are just up from the carpark and maybe we can spot some of those foxes or hares that Maureen told me live up here."

A smiling Marian with The O'Brien in tow was out of the car and heading up the road as Edward went to meet the arriving Garda.

Looking back to be sure that Marian was out of earshot; Edward motioned to the newly arrived patrol car and said to the young garda, "There's something dead in the boot of that car."

Looking grim, the young officer said, "I've just had the tags traced and the car was reported stolen in Dublin over a week ago."

Pulling a crowbar from the trunk, and tying a handkerchief over his nose and mouth to block out at least some of the smell he pried the boot open.

One look at the contents of the trunk sent the young officer racing to the nearest bushes and emptying the contents of his stomach.

Edward stood stoically staring at the decomposing corpse and said, "Looks like you guys have another murder on your hands."

Chapter 8

As the police vehicles continued to arrive and the area was cordoned off, Cat and The O'Brien kept Marian busy away from the scene that was unfolding below them in the parking lot. While the forensic team was busy extracting the remains from the boot of the car and preparing them for transfer to the morgue the rest of the officers were carefully searching the car and combing the area.

The chief inspector assigned to the case left the officers searching the car and walked over to where Edward was casually leaning against a tree. "Thanks for calling this in, sir. The patrolman said you have your family with you, so I'll try to make this as quick as possible. When did you first notice the car?"

"Actually, the car was probably here when we arrived this morning but we didn't notice anything until we returned about a few hours later. My daughter noticed the smell first and then O'Brien wouldn't stay away from the car."

"We'll need to speak to Mr. O'Brien, too."

Smiling Edward replied, "I'm afraid you won't get much out of him."

Looking irritated the inspector responded, "Why is that? Does he have something to hide or does he just not like police officers?"

"Umm...no...none of those. O'Brien's a dog."

Now, clearly embarrassed, the detective responded gruffly, "Just give your details to the officer over there and you're free to go. Just don't leave the area. We'll be wanting to take a full statement from you later."

After giving his details to the young patrolman who'd been first on the scene, Edward climbed into the Land Rover and drove it up the small lane towards the public toilets where Cat and Marian were playing fetch with O'Brien in the neighboring field.

As everyone climbed in the car and started down the road, Edward asked, "So ladies, how about we stop in Sligo for some lunch on the way home? I bet you guys are starving."

"Sounds good to me. How about you Marian? Are you hungry?" asked Cat.

"I sure am. Can we get mussels and chips, Da?"

"Sure. If that's what you want. Do you like mussels Cat?"

"I sure do."

"Well, I can guarantee you'll really enjoy your lunch. Sligo is famous throughout Ireland for their mussels."

Smiling Cat replied, "I am learning so much today I didn't know before about the county I now call home."

Looking back towards the car park Marian asked, "Da, why are all those Garda there?"

"Oh, it appears that car was stolen and just abandoned there."

Still looking back and crinkling up her nose, Marian continued, "What was that horrible smell?"

Thinking quickly Edward replied, "Well, it seems it was stolen with someone's groceries in the boot and they've been sitting in the sun so long that they've gone off," lied Edward as he nodded to Cat.

Picking up the hint, Cat responded as she held her nose, "That's what I smelled. Spoiled milk. Yuck!"

Acting satisfied with their answers, Marian turned her attention back to The O'Brien who now laid curled up with his head in her lap. Stroking his giant head she leaned close to his ear and whispered, " I think Da and Cat are telling porkies. You wouldn't have been so anxious to get in that boot if it was just spoiled milk would you?"

Hearing the buzz of his daughter's whisper Edward asked, "Did you say something Marian?"

"Just asking O'Brien what he wanted for lunch. He can't eat mussels you know."

"Well, what did his lordship say he wanted?" asked Edward.

Smiling as she stroked O'Brien's head Marian replied, " He said he would like a steak. A great big steak," as she held her hands in the air about a foot apart.

Traffic was light on the N15 as Edward drove the 23 miles to Sligo Town in very short time. Maneuvering through the streets he pulled into a car park and they headed to Marian's favorite pub for mussels. With Marian once again walking ahead with The O'Brien on his lead, Edward took advantage of the few moments of relative privacy and reached again for Cat's hand to tell her about the body in the car boot.

Smiling down into her blue eyes he said tenderly, "I hope the incident at the car park hasn't ruined the whole day for you."

Squeezing his hand Cat replied, "Absolutely not. It's a terrible thing but I'm not going to let it spoil an otherwise perfect day out."

Passing some of the High Street stores where Cat shopped for curtains and bedding for her cottage when she first moved to Ballysea, they found themselves walking beside the Garavogue river. Large baskets of colorful, cascading spring flowers hung from every lamppost that lined the walk along the river. Shaded benches were scattered

68

about the river's edge for the weary shoppers to sit and rest their weary feet.

"What a lovely area," remarked Cat as her eyes scanned the river walk.

Marian stood patiently waiting by the door of the pub and holding it open for her Da and Cat asked, "Shall we sit by the window table so O'Brien can look out at the river?"

Laughing Edward replied, "Absolutely and you can sit right beside him so you can cut up that enormous steak for him."

Once inside, Edward took their drinks order and went to the bar and returned with the menus.

Cat sat smiling and taking in the atmosphere of the pub. The crisp white table cloths and the shiny brass lamps were in sharp contrast to the dark paneled walls but combined with the fireplace against the far wall the large pub had a remarkably cozy atmosphere. While Cat was busy admiring her surroundings, Marian sat contently pointing out everything moving outside to The O'Brien.

Dropping into the wooden club chair next to Cat and passing her a menu, he asked, "So, shall it be the mussels or does something else on the menu take your fancy?"

Dropping the menu on the table Cat said, "Count me in. Make it three orders of mussels and chips and that enormous steak for himself over there."

While they were enjoying their lunch in Sligo Town, back in Ballysea Jeff was pacing the floor. Having just had a visit from Garda Burke informing him that he was looking for Cat and Edward to take their statements about the body they discovered in the car park at Benbulbin that morning, Jeff was beside himself. Unable to contain himself any longer, he crossed the lane to Maureen's and loudly banged on her door.

At the sound of the urgent banging, Maureen threw open the door exclaiming, "Whatever is the matter, Jeff?"

"Can I come in?" asked a panting Jeff.

"Of course. Sit down," replied Maureen as she pulled out a chair for the obviously upset Jeff.

70

"Have you heard about the murder?"

"Yes of course, I told you everything I knew about it this morning. Are you getting forgetful or has the jet lag got to you?" teased Maureen as she scurried around her kitchen preparing to fix him some tea.

"Tea?" she asked.

"Have you got anything stronger? And I think you best be getting two glasses because you might need some yourself," replied Jeff seriously.

Grabbing a bottle of Jameson from the kitchen cabinet and two glasses, Maureen sat opposite Jeff and asked, "What in the world has happened now?"

By the time Jeff had gotten half way through telling her about Edward and Cat discovering the dead body in the boot of the car, Maureen was reaching for the bottle to pour herself a second shot of whiskey.

"Dear lord, two bodies in less than a week. Things like this don't happen around here. Do you think the two could be related?" asked Maureen.

71

"Not sure. But according to the witnesses in Sligo, there were only two men on the boat and if this new body turns out to be the second man, then it stands to reason that the murderer is still on the loose."

With that comment, Maureen poured them each another glass of whiskey as they sat silently wondering what would happen next.

73

Chapter 9

It was late afternoon before Edward's car finally pulled up in front of Cat's cottage.

"Looks like you have company," said Edward pointing to the strange car parked beside Cat's cottage. Bringing his car to a stop on the lane, he climbed out and opened the back door letting The O'Brien and Marian out.

"Can I run over and see Caitlin and Miss Maureen while we're here?" pleaded Marian.

"Sure," replied Edward.

Quickly scanning the area, Cat called to Marian as she started across the lane, "Why don't you take The O'Brien with you. I'm sure he'd love a chance to stretch his legs after being cramped up in the back seat for so long."

Cat quickly gave The O'Brien the hand signal which he'd been taught and he immediately left her side and ambled over to where Marian waited. Looking over at Edward solemnly, Cat remarked, "With two murders so close to home, it might be a good idea not to let Marian go wandering off on her own for a while."

Edward suddenly looked concerned but before he could call Marian back Cat put her hand on his arm and nodded in the direction of the giant of a dog standing close to the young girl's side. "You don't have to worry about her right now. She is with The O'Brien and he won't leave her. Believe me, she'll come to no harm with him beside her."

As Marian and The O'Brien entered Maureen's cottage, Jeff came bursting out the door with a face resembling a thunder storm. Before either Cat or Edward even had a chance to greet him he shouted, "Where the Hell have you been? Garda Burke has been here looking for you and I've been worried sick."

Seeing the anguished look of worry on his face, Cat wrapped her arms around her best friend saying, "I'm so sorry Jeff. I had no idea you were coming or I would have been here to greet you."

Feeling contrite now, Jeff mumbled, "You didn't know because I didn't tell you. I heard on the news at home about the murder on the boat and was more than a little irritated you didn't call me as soon as it happened. Then I started worrying about you. So I booked a flight and came over."

Giving him another tight squeeze Cat replied, "I'm so sorry Jeff. I had no idea it would make the news in the States or I would have phoned you. Besides it doesn't have anything to do with me so I'm not in any danger."

Holding him at arm's length she smiled up into his worried eyes and said, "And you've been drinking, haven't you?"

Looking down and nodding his head like a naughty child, who'd been caught with his hand in the cookie jar, Jeff replied, "If you think I'm in bad shape, you should see Maureen."

This time it was Edward's turn to react as he sprinted across the lane yelling back to them, "I hope I'm not too late. I don't want Maureen to ask Marian about what happened today."

His knock at Maureen's door was answered by a grinning Caitlin and Marian as they each held a finger to their lips and pointed to the chair where Maureen sat passed out asleep.

Taking his daughter by the hand Edward whispered, "Why don't you let Miss Maureen sleep? She must have been working extremely hard today and needs her nap. You can come back to visit another day."

Nodding her head, Marian hugged Caitlin and waved goodbye and quietly shut the door behind them.

With The O'Brien still at Marian's side, father and daughter crossed the lane to Cat's cottage and knocked at the door.

Answering the door, a worried Jeff asked, "Everything alright?"

Smiling Edward winked at Jeff and said, "Yeah, fine. Seems Maureen has had a tiring day and is having herself a little unscheduled afternoon nap."

"I've put the kettle on. Jeff and I were getting ready to have a cup of tea would anyone else fancy a cup?" asked Cat.

"I'd love a cup," replied Edward as he pulled up a chair and reached over and slapped Jeff on the back.

Smiling at his friend Edward continued, "It's good to see you Jeff but you needn't worry about Cat. We keep a close eye on her. Don't we O'Brien?"

At the mention of his name, The O'Brien ambled over to the table, rested his chin on it and began making the little piggy grunting noises which never failed to make Cat laugh.

"Well, what are you trying to tell us big guy?" asked Edward as he reached over and patted O'Brien's head.

Laughing Cat said, "If we're sitting at the table that must mean food so he wants a biscuit."

Pulling a dog biscuit from the tin in the kitchen cabinet, Cat asked The O'Brien, "What do you say?"

The big animal immediately sat, raised one massive paw and loudly barked a "please."

With his biscuit safely in his mouth, he trotted off to the parlor and dropped down at Marian's feet.

As he watched the interaction between the big dog and the petite little girl, Jeff whispered to Edward, "Don't you think it's about time you started thinking about getting Marian her own dog. Take it from me, being an only child can be terribly lonely."

Edward held his finger to his lips and whispered back, "Cat and I have already discussed it. I've managed to locate a bitch up north and she'll be coming to visit The O'Brien the next time she comes into season. So with any luck Marian should have her own hound before Christmas."

Smiling from ear to ear, Jeff replied, "She'll be thrilled."

"To be honest, so will I. I've missed having a puppy for quite some time. I know we have our working collie but she prefers the barn to the house."

Draining the last sip of tea from his cup, Edward pushed back his chair and called to his daughter,

"Come on Marian. Time to head home sweetheart"

Giving one last hug to the now snoozing O'Brien, Marian quickly hugged Cat and Jeff and joined her father at the door.

Knowing the next few hours would be spent by the two friends catching up on the latest events, Edward called back from the open door and laughing said, "Stop up at the manor tomorrow if you two can spare time from your gossiping. We need to finalize those plans for the market re-opening."

Walking to the door, Jeff and Cat stood arm in arm as they waved goodbye to their friends. As she shut the door behind them Cat felt her eyes begin to well up with tears as she gazed at Jeff and remarked, "You never told me your childhood was lonely."

Shrugging his shoulders, Jeff started to clear the table as Cat stood waiting for a response.

When the silence grew too heavy for him to bear, Jeff turned to his friend and shrugged his shoulders. "It's really not something I like talking about. I prefer to live in the present and not dwell on the past."

Chapter 10

Cat was up at day break having slept on the sofa so Jeff could have the bed and sleep off his jetlag and over consumption of alcohol from the previous day. After putting the coffee on to brew, she grabbed her mac off the peg by the front door and touching her hand to her thigh silently signaled The O'Brien to her side.

Quietly closing the door behind her, she headed across the lane and down the small slope to the sandy beach below. Dropping down on her favorite rock she sat quietly observing the harbor and the town that rose up from it. No matter how hard she tried, her mind kept wandering back to the two dead men. She hoped Edward might have some word soon as to whether the two crimes were related. It was worrisome enough to have one murderer in the area then having to think about the possibility of more than one on the loose.

She was so deep in thought she didn't hear Maureen approach until she actually dropped down beside her on the rock.

"Jesus, Maureen. You nearly gave me a heart attack!" exclaimed Cat.

A laughing Maureen tried apologizing between giggles, "I'm sorry Cat. I thought you heard me coming. I guess it's lucky for you I wasn't the murderer."

"Strange you should say that. I was just sitting here wondering if there is one murderer or two. We don't know yet if the crimes are connected."

Quickly scanning the area Maureen replied, "I know and I don't mind telling you it's beginning to make me nervous. I never used to lock my doors during the day but I do now."

Cat was on her feet in a flash as Maureen asked, "What's the matter?"

Calling The O'Brien, Cat reached her hand down and pulled her friend to her feet and started up the small slope from the beach towards her cottage. "I left Jeff sleeping upstairs and didn't lock the door," called Cat over her shoulder.

Hurrying behind her, Maureen called to the fleeing back of her friend, "I'll be right there as soon as I stop at the house for the scones."

Jeff was just creeping down the stairs as Cat and The O'Brien entered her front door.

"Good Morning. How's the head?" asked Cat as she hurried to set the table.

Rubbing his temples with his finger tips to ease the pounding there Jeff muttered softly, "Morning. Thanks for letting me sleep in. I was out like a light last night and I feel much better this morning. Just no loud noises, please."

As Cat turned to pour the coffee she smiled at the sight of a messy haired, unshaven Jeff leaning down and pressing his face against The O'Brien's as he talked baby talk to the big animal.

Finally looking around and taking in the entire room Jeff asks, "Where's my girl Maureen and my scones?"

Before Cat had a chance to reply, the thumping of The O'Brien's tail announced the imminent arrival of Maureen.

Setting the scones down on the table, she and Jeff looked at each other and in unison asked, "How's your head?"

Laughing now, Jeff said, "I'm fine but I must say that you were absolutely rat-assed yesterday. I heard you had a nice afternoon nap though."

"Nap? More like I simply passed out where I sat. Thank goodness the children thought I'd been working too hard on the plans for the market reopening."

"Edward mentioned that yesterday," remarked Jeff as he reached for a scone.

Sliding the mugs of coffee over to her friends and taking one for herself, Cat finished filling The O'Brien's food dish and finally sat down.

"Edward wants us to stop up at the manor later today to go over some of the plans. Have you got time to go with us?" asked Cat as she looked over at Maureen.

"Sure, but I'll have to drive separately because I need to run into Sligo to pick up a few things." replied Maureen.

86

"When do you hope to have the market up and running," asked Jeff between bites.

"The permits are all approved and Edward and Jeff have almost all the stalls completed so it shouldn't be long now. I'm hoping we can set a date today," replied Cat.

"Why not consider having the first market on May Day?" asked Maureen between sips of her coffee.

Not being familiar with the Irish customs as practiced in the villages, Jeff asked, "Why May Day?"

"May Day or La Bealtaine is a Celtic Festival celebrated on the first Monday in May. Most of the shops and businesses will be closed. That way we wouldn't be taking any business away from the local shops and it would also allow the shop owners to try out the idea of having a stall at the market."

Excited by Maureen's suggestion, Cat remarked, "Great idea! We could have the stalls laid out in a circle around the town square and put a May Pole up in the middle. Make it a combination market and fair. That should bring the shoppers out."

The O'Brien suddenly vacated his place at the table and walking over and looking out the window began to wag his tag excitedly. That could mean only one thing. Company was coming.

Opening the door, Cat found Garda Burke with this hand raised in mid-air getting ready to knock.

"Morning Mike," called out Maureen and Jeff.

"Morning all. I was hoping to find Edward and Ryan here this morning. Are you expecting them?" asked Mike as he reached in his pocket and unwrapped the chunks of beef his Uncle Jim, the butcher, always sent to The O'Brien.

As she watched The O'Brien gently take the offered treats from the young policeman Cat replied, "Actually no Mike, we are going to meet them at the Manor later today to discuss the market. What's up?"

"We have a preliminary identification on the body found in the boot of the stolen car. The man's next of kin is due to arrive here later today to confirm the identification. I was going to ask if they could be there."

Jeff asked, "Do you think his death is related to the body from the boat?"

"We can't say for sure. All we know at this point is that he was a young man with no previous criminal record. He was identified through a missing persons' report filed by his sister in Dublin."

"Did the car belong to his family?" asked Jeff.

"No. According to his sister, they didn't own a car and her brother had some type of issues which would have prevented him from driving," replied Mike.

Always the lawyer, Jeff replied, "Then we can safely assume someone else drove the car and left this young man's body in the boot. Have they established a time of death?"

"According to the coroner, he was murdered the morning before the storm and his body was placed in the boot of the car immediately after death?"

"How in the world can he tell that?" asked Maureen.

"It had something to do with the amount of blood in the boot of the car. He died from multiple stab wounds. From the defense wounds on his hands it appears he tried to fight off his attacker," replied Mike.

A pensive Cat shook her head and said, "So sad for his family."

"Why not give Edward a call from here and see if they would rather meet up with us here later after they help Mike out in Sligo with the next of kin?" suggested Jeff.

"Good idea. Mike why don't you talk to him first and then pass the phone to me and we'll make our arrangements," replied Cat.

After a brief phone call to the manor, Edward and Ryan agreed to meet Garda Burke in Sligo at the coroner's office and then stop off at Cat's before returning home.

Once all their company left, Cat and Jeff sat comfortably discussing all the latest gossip from home when Jeff grew unusually quiet.

"What's wrong Jeff? I can tell something is bothering you," asked Cat as she leaned over and slipped her arm through his.

"I feel terrible about being so abrupt with you the other night when you asked me about my childhood. You've shared everything about your life with me and I haven't done the same with you."

"That's OK Jeff. If it's something you don't want to talk about then I respect that. You're my friend and nothing you could ever say to me is going to change that," replied Cat gazing into the troubled face of her dearest friend.

Raising his face and gazing into Cat's worried eyes Jeff continued, "I think I'm ready to tell you now."

Cat sat quietly holding Jeff's hand as he shared with her the story of his early years. Cat had always been surprised Jeff was an only child since he had been born into an Irish Catholic family. She had just assumed like her own mother, Jeff's mother was unable to have more children.

"Do you know anything about Asperger's Syndrome?" asked Jeff.

Cat nodded, "It's a type of Autism isn't it?"

"Well, yes but a very high functioning type. When I was young I wasn't well coordinated and was somewhat socially awkward around other children. I preferred to play by myself and I would be somewhat fixated on certain toys. As I got older, I would become absorbed with certain topics to the exclusion of everything else and that's all I would want to talk about. It drove my father nuts. I was an embarrassment to him. I actually remember overhearing him tell my mother there would be no more children because he didn't want to take the chance of having another retarded child."

Cat's face grew red and her mouth dropped open in shock as she tightly griped her closest friend's hand exclaiming, "What a horrible thing to say! I bet he was eating those words when you won the scholarship to law school and graduated at the top of your class."

"I wouldn't know Cat. He walked out on us when I was twelve. I've had no contact with him since."

"Do you know if he's still alive?" she asked.

"Don't know and frankly don't care. He broke my mother's heart when he left and even though she never showed it, I always felt like it was my fault."

Putting both arms around her friend all Cat could say was, "It wasn't and I'm sure your mother never felt it was."

Quickly breaking her embrace, Jeff was on his feet and heading for the door pulling Cat behind him.

"Whoa, where are we going?" asked Cat.

"Fish and chips! I fancy fish and chips drenched in vinegar and a walk on the beach. Come on O'Brien," called Jeff.

As Cat closed the cottage door behind them, she looked up to see Jeff wipe a tear from his cheek. It had taken a lot for the very private Jeff to share his past with her and now he wanted to move on and forget it.

Chapter 11

It had just gone past 1:00 pm as Cat and Jeff finished their fish and chips and sat contently waiting for The O'Brien to finish his romp when they noticed three people approaching from the village. When they grew closer, Cat recognized Edward and Ryan Granville walking slowly towards her cottage with a tall, slender lady between them.

"It looks like we're getting company. We better go greet them," remarked Cat as she let out a shrill whistle calling O'Brien.

Climbing to his feet, Jeff reached a hand down to Cat and said, "Thank you for listening. I think I feel better with you knowing."

Smiling Cat said, "That's what friends do."

Hand in hand with The O'Brien trailing behind them the two friends climbed the small rise from the beach to greet their friends.

Edward was first to greet them and introduce the stranger to them.

"Cat and Jeff, may I introduce Briana Collins. Briana is in town from Dublin to identify her brother's remains."

Jeff was first to reach for the pretty raven haired woman's hand to offer his condolences, "I'm so sorry for your loss. If there is anything we can do, please don't hesitate to ask."

Before she had a chance to reply, Ryan said, "It's been a rough morning so maybe some coffee and friendly company."

Steering them towards the house, Cat responded, "Of course. Won't you come in?"

As she entered the house, Briana's eyes swept over the small cottage and smiling said in the softest of voices, "This reminds me of my grandmother's cottage...so warm and comforting."

As she sat at the table, The O'Brien wandered over and circled the stranger before returning to Cat's side to sit and watch the stranger.

"What a beautiful hound!" Briana exclaimed. "What's his name?"

"He's called The O'Brien." Reaching down and stroking The O'Brien's head, Cat thought to herself, 'Someone is certainly acting strange.' Normally, The O'Brien sensed when people were in need and tried to comfort them.

Looking up with tears welling in her doe-like eyes, Briana responded, "Shamus would have loved him. He always wanted a hound but once we moved to Dublin our apartment was too small and between school and work my schedule was too busy to give a dog the care it deserves."

Pouring the freshly brewed coffee into the waiting mugs, Cat asked, "Shamus is your brother?"

Nodding her head in response, Briana continued, "My brother had developmental issues so when our parents died he came to live with me. He was what some people would call 'slow' but always happy and trusting. I'm afraid his trusting nature may have brought him to this."

Seeing her hands begin to shake, Jeff quickly changed the subject, "So what prompted your move to Dublin, Ms. Collins?"

97

Glancing up from her coffee, Briana smiled and replied, "Please call me Briana. You and your wife have been kind enough to invite me into your home, so first names please."

Trying to stifle a laugh Jeff replied, "Oh, sorry for laughing but Cat and I are best friends. I'm just visiting her from the States. We aren't married."

Blushing prettily Briana replied, "Oh, sorry. I shouldn't have assumed but to answer your question, I was at Art and Design University and I'm a designer now."

Before Cat could ask her what she designed, The O'Brien stood and went to the door signaling he wanted out. As she rose from the table to excuse herself, Edward spoke for the first time since entering the cottage, "Wait up Cat, I'll walk with you."

As Edward and Cat made their way up the hill to the open fields above the cliff, he told her about the traumatic visit to the morgue earlier in the day.

"She is totally devastated and she has no idea how he ended up in the boot of that car. Mike was the officer assigned to question her but we suggested she be given some time to collect herself and he agreed to come by your house and ask her a few questions. She did mention on the way over here the only hint of something different in her brother's behavior was a sudden interest in his appearance."

"Sounds like he may have found a lady friend," responded Cat thoughtfully as she watched The O'Brien running through the field looking for anything that moved.

"Yes, that's what I thought too and then I remembered those men from the boat had been overheard talking about their female boss and wondered if the two incidents could be related."

"Yes, I must admit I thought that and the boat was registered in Dublin so there is that link there too."

Tiring from his run and panting heavily, O'Brien was ready to return home.

As they walked down the narrow well- worn path to the cottages below, Cat remarked, " The

O'Brien sure acted strange with Briana. Did you notice?"

"Not really. What do you mean Cat?"

"The O'Brien never seems to meet a stranger and he always seems so instinctively gentle with people in need but he was unusually stand-offish with Briana."

Looking down at the gentle giant walking closely by his mistress' side, Edward replied, "I wasn't paying attention but remember we've just come from the morgue and it may have been the scent of death or the lab chemicals that put him off."

Shrugging her shoulders, Cat replied, "I never thought of that. That's probably what it was." Quickly changing the subject she continued, "Oh, we were going to finalize the plans with you today for having the opening day for the market on May Day but that can wait."

Reaching over and grabbing her hand, Edward smiled down at her and asked, "Over coffee in the morning?"

"Sure. That'll still give us two weeks to finalize everything."

As they approached the cottage, they were met by Mike and a female Garda just exiting their patrol car. The O'Brien was the first to greet them as the giant of a dog gently stood on his hind legs and placed his paws on Mike's shoulders and looking down promptly licked his face.

"Please O'Brien, I'm on official business today," he said as he laughed and tried without success to disengage himself from what could only be described as a wolfhound hug.

"No treats today," called Cat as The O'Brien slowly climbed off of the young Garda.

"Cat and Edward, this is Garda Boyle. It's policy to send a female liaison officer out with the officer in charge, if he is male, when questioning a female."

"Shall we go in?" asked Cat as she swung open the cottage door.

The three remaining occupants had moved into Cat's sitting room and were now discussing the differences between Irish and American judicial systems and Cat could tell by the look in Jeff's eyes he was more than a little interested in the lady.

Seeing Garda Burke and the female officer enter, Ryan and Jeff excused themselves and moved into the kitchen to give the officers some privacy while questioning Briana.

Finding the victim's sister had little information that would help them in their investigation the two officers once again offered their condolences and headed for the door.

Opening the door for them, Edward asked, "Where does it go from here Mike?"

"The case will be turned over to the Dublin Garda Station since the car was stolen from there."

Mike looked at Edward and nodded toward the door signaling for him to step outside. He continued in a low voice no one inside would hear, "We're still waiting for more tests on the remains to find out exactly where the murder was committed."

"I see. Thanks for the information Mike. Ryan offered to put Ms. Collins up for the night at the manor so she isn't alone tonight. If you think of anything else you need to ask her she'll be there until about noon tomorrow when she plans to drive home to make her brother's final arrangements."

"That's kind of you. She shouldn't be alone and she certainly shouldn't drive back today while she is so upset. Thankfully, I don't think we'll need to trouble her again," replied Mike as he waved goodbye and joined his fellow Garda in the patrol car.

As he turned to re-enter Cat's cottage, Edward caught a glimpse of a curtain moving at Maureen's kitchen window and thought, 'It's not like Maureen not to check if everything is alright when she sees the Garda here. Wonder why she hasn't popped over?' Shrugging his shoulders, he walked through the door to find everyone still talking amiably and waiting for a lull in the conversation said, " Perhaps we should head back to the manor so Briana could relax before dinner."

Walking their guests to the door, Cat asked." Are we still on for coffee in the morning?'

Waving back as they walked down the lane, Edward responded, "Sure, come for breakfast if you like. I'll let Mrs. O'Malley to expect company."

Eager to see Briana again Jeff was the first to respond, "We'd be delighted." Looking directly at Briana he continued, "I look forward to more discussions on the difference in the Irish and American lifestyles."

Chapter 12

Cat had barely crawled out of bed and staggered down the stairs when The O'Brien's wagging tail and soft whimper alerted her that Maureen was on her way across the narrow lane that separated their cottages. Running her fingers through her still uncombed hair Cat wondered what was bringing Maureen to her door so early this morning. Quickly unlocking the door and holding a finger to her lips as she pointed to the curled up lump under the blanket on her sofa.

"Morning. It was a late night and Jeff's still out like a light. I think he has taken a fancy to that Ms Briana Collins who was here yesterday after identifying her brother at the morgue," whispered Cat as she set about making the coffee.

Raising her eyebrow Maureen replied, "Ms. Briana Collins, really?"

Turning away from fixing the coffee to face her friend, Cat asked, "OK, what is it? We've been friends long enough for me to know when something isn't sitting quite right with you."

"Maybe it's nothing but when I saw her walking up the lane towards your cottage with Edward and Ryan yesterday, I could have sworn that I recognized her. I just can't place from where at the moment."

Pouring the freshly brewed coffee, Cat responded, "I wouldn't let it trouble you. They say everyone has at least one double."

"I know, but I hate when I can't remember things. Must be getting old," sighed Maureen.

The fragrant aroma of the coffee soon had Jeff awake and clad only in pajama bottoms wandering into the kitchen. Playfully poking him in the abs, Maureen smiled and said, "Very nice! Now get your shirt on before you get people talking about Cat and I having coffee with half naked men."

Beaming widely, Jeff grabbed his undershirt and pulling it over his head, dropped down on the nearest chair and reaching for his coffee asked Maureen, "Are you coming up to the manor with us this morning? We've been invited for breakfast."

"I have a meeting at school this morning with Caitlin's teacher so I'll have to pass but you're in for a treat. Mrs. O'Malley puts on a fantastic breakfast spread with all the fixings."

"I can hardly wait," replied Jeff as he tilted his head back and finished his coffee and stood up to head upstairs.

Smiling broadly he yelled back over his shoulder, "I hate to leave such charming company but I'm off for a shower. Have to keep up appearances. See you this afternoon Maureen."

Soon as they heard the bathroom door shut, both women burst out in giggles.

"I do believe you are right Cat. Someone seems smitten," remarked Maureen.

Cat sat pensively smiling as she thought about Maureen's earlier remarks about Briana's identity and The O'Brien's strange behavior towards the woman.

Noticing the look on her friend's face, Maureen asked, "Is something bothering you, Cat?"

Shaking her head she replied, "It's just one of the many disadvantages of being a writer. You tend to have an overactive imagination."

"You're upset by what I said about Ms. Collins, aren't you?" asked Maureen.

"Well, maybe just a little and The O'Brien wasn't exactly what I would call friendly with her yesterday.'

With the mention of his name, The O'Brien was up from his bed in the lounge and beside his mistress. Resting his big head in her lap, he stared up at her troubled face then gently climbed to where he could rest his big head against her cheek.

Wrapping her arms tightly around her beloved hound, Cat gently stroked his head and said, "It's alright big fellow. I'm fine. It's nothing that you need to worry yourself about."

Climbing down to sit closely pressed up against her side, the worried expression in the big dog's eyes remained. Instinctively, he knew when something was bothering his mistress and he would be even more vigilant when strangers were near her. She was his family now and although naturally docile and affectionate, when someone a wolfhound loved was threatened his breed would fight to the death to protect them.

Maureen was first to break the silence and quickly changing the subject asked, "Do you think you'll have time to speak to Edward and Ryan about the market plans?"

"That's the plan. The stalls are all ready and we have plenty of people interested in them. I think at last count we had 5 available for late comers. I'll need to ask them about getting a May Pole set up and arrange for some entertainment."

Finishing her coffee and giving The O'Brien a final pat on his head Maureen said, "I best be getting home and get ready to meet with Caitlin's teacher. I'll talk with you later."

Following her friend to the door, Cat grimaced as she noticed that the day which had dawned bright had now turned dreary with that fine mist that seem to cling to everything like tiny slivers of iron to a magnet.

Standing in front of her mirror, she touched up her lip gloss and began to brush her hair. Groaning loudly and throwing down her hair brush Cat loudly exclaimed "I don't know why I even bother with my hair on days like this. As soon as I walk outside it'll all turn to frizz."

Bounding down the stairs and to her side Jeff used his hip to bump Cat away from the only mirror in the cottage exclaiming, "You look beautiful just the way you are, besides Edward has seen you looking much worse."

"I beg your pardon," replied Cat trying to keep a stern face. "And who might you be dolling yourself up for this morning? As if I didn't already know."

"Am I that transparent?" asked Jeff as he suddenly dropped his comb and looked over at Cat.

Laughing now at the worried face of her dearest friend, Cat replied, "Only to someone that has known you for as long as I have. Don't worry. I am sure Brianna doesn't know that you have any romantic interest in her."

Shaking his head Jeff groaned, "I'm doomed. I haven't a clue about how relationships are meant to progress. I've always been so busy between college and building a successful law firm that I haven't had the time or inclination to have one and now when I finally find someone that appeals to me I don't know where to start."

"Just be yourself Jeff and she can't help but like you," assured Cat as they made their way out the door with The O'Brien trailing behind.

Just making his way up the lane from the harbor, Garda Burke called, "Good Morning! Are you off to the manor already? No Maureen this morning? "

"Yes, we were invited for breakfast at the manor. And no, Maureen's off to school this morning to meet with Caitlin's teacher so not today. Any news on the murders?" asked Jeff.

"No news yet. Seems like we've really come up against a brick wall. The police in Dublin haven't been able to get any further with the death of Ms. Collin's brother either. Whoever stole the car and killed the young man was very careful not to leave

112

any prints and we couldn't find a murder weapon so either the perpetrator took it with him or it's at the bottom of the sea somewhere. It's odd though," replied Mike pushing his cap back away from his face.

"What's odd Mike?" asked Cat.

"According to the Dublin police, when there's drug smuggling going on there seems to be an indication of that by an increase of the drugs available on the streets. Lately it seems quite the opposite. The clinics have been having more addicts showing up looking for Methadone because there's a shortage of drugs on the streets," replied Mike.

"Maybe they were being smuggled to the continent," offered Jeff.

"That's one theory but why take the risk and expense when there is so much demand here," replied Mike.

"No idea but we better get on or we'll miss Mrs. O'Malley's world famous breakfast," said Jeff.

At the mention of the word breakfast, The O'Brien was at the car door tail wagging excitedly waiting to climb into the back seat.

Laughing Cat grabbed Jeff's arm and said, "Someone must be hungry. Best get our friend in the back seat before he takes off and runs to the manor on his own."

Waving goodbye to Garda Burke, the three companions climbed into the car and headed out of town for the short drive to the manor and breakfast.

No sooner had the car come to a halt and the back door opened, than The O'Brien was off through the open kitchen door in search of Marian and breakfast.

Laughing Cat said, "I'm not sure what he loves more, that child or the thought of breakfast."

Linking her arm through Jeff's, Cat steered him through the open door following the delicious aroma wafting from the kitchen.

Entering the large kitchen they were greeted with the sight of Mrs. O'Malley's rather large bottom as she bent over the ancient Aga taking scones from the oven. Yelling back over her shoulder Mrs. O'Malley called, "Everyone is in the dining room. Go on through."

Following the sound of laughter and Marian squeals of delight, Jeff and Cat made their way into the formal dining room to find Marian cuddling with The O'Brien by the fire and the adults sitting at the massive table enjoying their coffees.

"Good Morning everyone. Looks like we're just in time, Mrs. O'Malley's just bringing in the scones." said Jeff as he pulled a chair out and sat down opposite Briana.

Cat could only stand and stare at the immense amount and variety of food on the table. Finally she said in a hushed voice, "Are we expecting more people?"

Shaking his head, Edward replied, "Not that I know of, well maybe Mike Burke, why?"

Watching the two brothers as they began to pile enormous amounts of food onto their plates, Cat just smiled across to Briana who was now also trying to stifle a smile and replied, "No reason."

Taking advantage of the break in conversation created by the men enjoying their breakfast, Cat presented her plans for the May Day market opening. While the response from the men were only nods of agreement while they continued to shovel food into their mouths. Cat's ideas drew an animated response from Briana.

 "A May Day Fete and Market…that sounds wonderful. Did I tell you that I design and sell my own jewelry? I wasn't planning on having a show until the autumn but this might help me keep my mind off things in the meantime. I would love to have a stall if there any still available for vendors," said Briana.

Jumping at the chance to see Briana again, Jeff finally put down his fork and responded, "I'm sure we can find a spot for you. Can't we Cat?", he pleaded.

"Of course, we have a few stalls available and no one is selling jewelry so I think it would make a great addition.

Chapter 13

May Day dawned bright and clear as Cat and Maureen with The O'Brien by their side moved quickly through the market place checking on the flourish of activity as the stall owners set out their wares.

Rounding the corner to the center of the market square, The O'Brien took off in a trot to greet Edward, Ryan and Garda Mike Burke as they put on the finishing touches of the May Pole.

"Morning ladies! Look like an talamh torthach' is smiling on us today," called Mike as he helped unfurl the colorful streamers attached to the top of the pole.

"An talamh torthach'?" asked Cat?

Smiling brightly, Maureen replied, "mother nature."

"Ahhh...I guess that I need to take a class in Gaelic soon," said Cat.

"Everything under control at the stalls Cat?" asked Edward.

Cat waved her arm around in the direction of the stalls that formed a semi-circle around the May Pole. "Look for yourself! It looks like a everyone is ready and the crowds are just starting to arrive."

Soon the May Day festivities were well under way allowing Cat and Maureen to take a break and head for the refreshment tent.

Glancing over toward Briana's stall, Maureen stopped abruptly and stared at the well-dressed stranger crossing the square and approaching Briana's stall.

Poking Cat in the ribs she pointed to Briana's stall, " Uh oh, could that be competition going towards Briana's stall? Jeff won't be pleased."

Soon as his mistress turned to look in the direction of the stall, The O'Brien's attention focused on the stranger and as Cat and Maureen turned and started towards to refreshment tent, he stood his ground and continued to stare.

Cat had only gone a few feet when she realized The O'Brien wasn't following. Turning back, she called to him but instead of coming to her side as usual, he just lowered his big head and continued to stand his ground and stare at the stranger.

"What's with him?" asked Maureen shielding her eyes from the sun and looking in the direction of The O'Brien.

Shaking her head Cat replied, "I don't know. I've only seen him behave like that a couple times before and both times something bad was about to happen."

"Oh lord. I hope not," was all Maureen could say as she quickly crossed herself.

"We better wander over to Briana's stall. Maybe that will settle him down. One thing for sure is that we won't be getting our tea now because he isn't going to budge until he goes where he wants," said Cat as she reached over and patted The O'Brien saying, "Come on then stubborn. Let's go see what has you all worked up."

Briana was wrapping up a purchase for another customer at the back of the stall as the stranger approached Jeff at the front.

"May I help you," asked Jeff.

120

"I was in the area and stopped by to offer Ms. Collins my condolences. I've been out of the country and I didn't hear of her loss until I returned."

At the sound of her name, Briana turned with a confused look on her face, "It's Mr. Vincent, isn't it? I'm sorry I didn't recognize you at first. It's been so long since we last met."

"Jeff, Mr. Vincent was one of our teachers at school. I haven't seen him in years. "

"Nice to meet you, Mr. Vincent," replied Jeff.

Just nodding at Jeff, Mr. Vincent continued, "Just call me Sam," before turning his attention back to Briana.

"I was so sorry to learn about your brother's death. I remember how close your family was. The newspaper was very vague. What happened?"

Wiping a tear from her eye, Brianna reached over and touched Jeff's arm and asked, "Can you watch my stall for a few minutes? I'm afraid if I talk about Seamus here that I might break down completely in front of the customers."

"Sure Briana. Why don't you and your friend go have some tea and catch up."

Wandering over from the direction of the refreshment tent to the stall and finding Jeff manning it alone Cat asked, "Where's Briana disappeared to?"

Jeff's explanation was abruptly interrupted by a sudden loud tapping on the counter. The three friends turned and stared at the newcomer in shocked silence.

"Hello, I was expecting to find my sister minding her stall and not some handsome man."

"Sister?" asked Jeff astonished at the similarity between the two.

Smiling widely now, the stranger replied, "I'm Brenna, Briana's twin. I'm surprised she didn't mention she had a sister.

Reaching for the dark haired beauty's outstretched hand Jeff responded, "Jeff Hunter. I'm just minding the stall while your sister is catching up with her old teacher, Mr. Vincent."

"Really? I haven't seen him in years. Do you know where they went?"

"I thought they were going toward the refreshment tent but my friends here said they've just come from that direction and didn't see them."

"Well, thank you. I'll have a wander around and see if I can find her," said Brenna as she winked boldly at Jeff and walked away.

Walking out of view of the stall, Brenna immediately reached into her purse and pulled out her mobile and dialing the number said, "Where the hell are you Sam? You told her what? Stay right there. I'm on my way."

Skirting the beach and making for the cliff path, she headed for the spot where her sister now lay bound and gagged behind one of the standing stones.

Kneeling in front of her, Brenna gently pulled the gag from her mouth and sweetly asked, "I left some loose stones in a plastic baggie with your jewelry supplies. Where are they Briana now?"

123

Ignoring her sister's question Briana asked, "What have you done? How could you hurt Seamus? He was our baby brother."

"Yes, he was my brother too but he wasn't the innocent you thought he was. He was in on this heist too. Said he needed money to take out his new lady friend and said you were too tight to give him any, but at the last minute, he decided that he didn't want to be a bad boy and was going to the Garda. It was either silence him or spend the rest of my life in jail and I wasn't going back to jail for that idiot. So answer my question. Where are my stones?"

Finally realizing what stones her sister was asking about and what she had done with them, Briana looked down toward Ballysea and her market stall.

"So where's the diamonds?" asked Sam.

Following her sister's eyes Brenna replied, "Oh Christ, probably being sold at her stall to the local yokels at this very moment. I hid them with Briana's costume jewelry because she said she wasn't having a show until Autumn. When I went to her house to retrieve them I found a note saying

124

she was having a stall here today. That's why I told you to wait for me here. No, but you had to take things into your own hands and run your big mouth. Now what am I supposed to do about my sister? "

Sneering, Sam replied, "The same thing you did to your brother unless you fancy spending the rest of your life in jail."

Understanding now that she was in mortal danger, Briana tried desperately to call for help before Sam quickly gagged her again.

"Keep her quiet Sam. We need to figure out how we're going to get those diamonds back before they're all sold as paste."

Tightening the gag, Sam replied, "Don't worry. No one could hear her from up here especially with all the commotion down there."

Normally that would have been true but Sam hadn't counted on The O'Brien's sensitive ears.

Back at the stall, The O'Brien's massive head whipped rapidly around and in a move unlike anything Cat ever witnessed, the gentle animal barred his teeth and took off at full speed toward the beach.

Laughing Jeff asks, "Sea gulls?"

"No. Someone is in terrible trouble. Get help!" yelled Cat as she took off after the big dog.

"I'll go for Edward and Ryan. Maureen try to find Garda Burke." shouted Jeff.

Panting for her breath Cat finally reached the top of the cliff to witness a bound and gagged Briana in the grips of the stranger with The O'Brien circling him teeth bared.

As Cat watched helplessly, Vincent pushed Briana in front of the menacing hound and took off down the path toward the village with The O'Brien in hot pursuit herding him right into the waiting arms of Edward, Ryan and Jeff.

Kneeling beside Briana, Cat quickly began untying her only to be grabbed by the throat from behind by Brenna.

"You should have minded your own business. Now there'll be two of you going over this cliff today," sneered Brenna as she began to drag Cat toward the cliff edge.

Just as she turned to position herself to push Cat over the edge, a deep throaty growl greeted her ears from between her and the cliff edge. The O'Brien had worked his way behind her and now stood head lowered in full attack stance. Slowly backing away from the threatening fangs, Brenna let go of Cat and holding her hands in the air began to back away from the still approaching O'Brien. Incensed by the brutal murder of her brother Briana grabbed her sister from behind by her hair and the twins became locked in a death dance dangerously close to the edge and sudden death.

Struggling to her feet Cat watched in horror as Brenna's foot slipped on the damp ground and she went over the edge. Arms flailing she managed to grab onto an outgrowth of brush on the cliff wall and land on a small ledge temporarily breaking her fall. Before she could be lost to the rocks below, Briana dropped down on her stomach and reached for her sister's outstretched hand and gripping her wrist shouted, "Help me someone! I can't hold her much longer. We need to pull her up."

Moving quickly to her side, Cat tried desperately to help Briana pull her sister to safety.

Unable to budge her, Cat raced over and grabbed the rope that had been used to restrain Briana and fashioning a halter looped it across The O'Brien's chest and shoulders then passed it down the cliff wall yelling, "Slip it around you the best you can. We'll pull you up."

"OK, I've done it. Please hurry! This ledge is beginning to crumble."

Racing back to where The O'Brien stood waiting, Cat grabbed the top of the halter and yelled back to Briana, "Get ready to grab her arm. We're only going to get one shot at this! We're going to pull now."

The O'Brien seemed to understand exactly what was needed from him because as soon as Cat said pull the big dog dug in and began pulling with all his might. Just as it appeared that he could go no farther Briana yelled, "I almost have her. Just a little more!"

"Just one more pull big fellow," called Cat as she ran back to the cliff edge.

Looking back at his mistress and sensing the urgency in her voice, he dug his hind legs in and surged forward one more time. It was just far enough for Briana and Cat to grab Brenna firmly by her arms and pull her to safety.

It was just at that very moment that Edward, Ryan and Jeff arrived after leaving Sam Vincent in the custody of Garda Burke. As Jeff went to help Briana, Edward called desperately to Cat.

"Cat. Come quick. It's The O'Brien."

Pushing herself up from her knees, Cat stood and turned to where Edward and Ryan were leaning over the prostrate dog.

"Oh no. O'Brien!" she screamed as she ran to his side tears streaming from her eyes. Wrapping her arms around him she whispered gently, "You'll be alright big fellow. We'll get you home." Hearing her calming voice The O'Brien tried struggling to his feet only to collapse again.

The two brothers gently lifted the big dog and began carefully carrying him down the cliff towards Cat's cottage.

Maureen was just on her way up with old Doctor Summers, medical bag in hand, when she spotted the brothers carrying The O'Brien down towards Cat's cottage.

Running ahead she yelled, "Is everyone else OK?"

Cat looked back and seeing Jeff and Briana with her sister to tow called back to Maureen, "Everyone except The O'Brien. Can you get the vet?"

Waving his hand, Doc Summer replied calmly, "The vet's up at Hillside Farm but I'll have a look at the big fellow."

Running ahead and opening the cottage door, Maureen and Doc waited for his patient to arrive as Jeff and Garda Burke escorted Brenna and Sam to jail.

With The O'Brien gently laid on his dog bed, Doc pulled his stethoscope from his black bag and began to listen to O'Briens heart and lungs.

"Well, his heart rate is a little fast but that's normal if he has been exerting himself and his lungs are clear. What was he doing right before he collapsed?"

After explaining how The O'Brien was harnessed and pulling Brenna up from the cliff the village GP nodded and began to run his hands over The O'Brien's legs.

As his knowledgeable hands ran over The O'Brien's hind quarters he looked up and nodded at the worried faces watching his every move.

"Just as I suspected, I think I've found the problem but we'll need to wait for the vet to return so he can confirm my diagnosis."

Tears beginning to stream down her face again Cat asked, "What do you think it is? Will he be alright?"

Smiling now as he patted The O'Briens head Doc replied, "I think he has either pulled or strained his back leg muscles and that's why he is staying down. You know, animals have better sense than a lot of humans when it comes to knowing when it's time to rest an overworked muscle."

Overjoyed, Cat flung herself at the aging GP and hugging him tightly asked, "How can I ever thank you?"

"Oh, I think that was thanks enough," replied the blushing old gentleman.

Maureen could have sworn the sound of sighs of relief from everyone gathered around The O'Brien could have been heard all the way to Sligo.

Chapter 14

Nearly a week passed before The O'Brien was steady enough on his feet to gingerly begin chasing the pesky sea gulls from the beach but during that time Cat's cottage was a virtual beehive of activity. Edward and Ryan joined Cat, Jeff and Maureen for their morning coffee and Garda Burke stopped by daily to keep them up to date on the investigation . Once the word got out around the village of The O'Brien's heroics, neighbor after neighbor stopped in to check on his recovery and bring him little treats.

It was on the second day, that Garda Burke had details of the two prisoner's confessions.

"Vincent has made a full confession to the murder of the unidentified man from the boat," said Mike Burke as he reached for the cup of coffee that Cat had placed in front of him.

"What about the other man that was on the boat whose body wasn't found?" asked Cat.

"There was no other body. We were sent on a wild goose chance deliberately set up by Vincent. He was the other man on the boat. According to his confession, he argued with his accomplice after drinking at the pub and the other guy swallowed a baggy containing a small quantity of the diamonds. This incensed Vincent and he slashed the man's throat."

Edward put down his coffee and raising his eyebrow asked, "Why dismember him like that?"

Mike continued, "He wanted us to assume that it was a drug smuggling gone wrong and he was quite right when it came to that. We were not even considering anything other than drugs. We never suspected diamonds."

Jeff asked, "Had there been any reports of diamond thefts before the incident?"

"No, there hadn't been any reported thefts but Brenna's confession cleared that up for us."

Suddenly Maureen jumped to her feet and grabbing Maureen's hand said, "Now I remember why Briana looked familiar to me. I saw Brenna's picture in the paper about five years ago. Wasn't she the mistress of some big time jewel thief, Mike?"

Smiling Mike replied, "You have a good memory. Just wish you had remembered it sooner. Yes, she was and she spent time in prison for being involved in one of his schemes. She actually stole the diamonds from her old boyfriend after spending the night with him and drugging him. Because they were stolen in the first place, he could hardly report the theft. She hoped to get them sold and leave the country quickly before he sent his gang after her."

Shaking her head, all Cat could say was, "And for this she murdered her own brother."

"Yes. She's confessed to killing Seamus but claims he came at her with his knife and in the struggle that ensued he was stabbed through the heart and died instantly," replied Mike.

"Then why all the other wounds?" asked Ryan.

"Another ploy to throw us off track she claims," replied Mike shrugging his shoulders in disbelief. "Frankly, I think she has a taste for killing. She sure wasn't going to hesitate throwing Briana and Cat over the cliff. I hate to think what could have happened if The O'Brien hadn't been there."

A sudden chill passed over Cat and shivering she exclaimed, "Felt like someone just walked across my grave."

Slipping his arm around her shoulders, Edward said, "Not while you have The O'Brien and me by your side."

No sooner were those words out of his mouth than the room grew quiet and everyone turned to stare at Cat as her face took on a rosy glow.

Clearing his throat, Jeff quickly changed the subject, "Speaking of The O'Brien, when is he to be introduced to his lady friend?"

With the blush slowly disappearing Cat quickly responded, "As soon as his DNA test comes back."

"DNA test for a dog?" asked Mike.

"Yes Mike. Since The O'Brien more or less adopted me and I don't know anything about where he came from or have his AKC papers proving he is a pure breed, the owner of the bitch asked that we have a DNA test to prove he is a full breed Wolfhound," replied Cat.

"As long as we have the pup in time for Christmas that's all that matters," added Edward smiling.

"I can't wait to see her face on Christmas morning," said Jeff.

Maureen was first to reach across for Jeff's hand as she asked, "Does that mean you'll be spending the holidays with us?"

"Yes, if Cat will have me," replied Jeff.

"Of course I will," exclaimed Cat..

The rest of the morning was spent by the six friends cheerfully talking about the holiday season six months away as all thoughts of murders were forgotten...at least for the time being.

Epilogue

Once again peace had returned to the sleepy little fishing village of Ballysea. The summer passed all too quickly for Cat and The O'Brien as days grew shorter and the weather cooler.

Jeff returned to Annapolis and his law practice a week after the arrests but not before spending a week in Dublin where the shy lawyer and Briana got to know each other better.

The village markets continued throughout the summer and had proven such a success that a Christmas market was already being planned.

Cat and Edward continued to spend time together over the summer as their relationship, like the temperatures, grew warmer.

As for The O'Brien...well his DNA test confirmed that he was indeed a full bred Irish Wolfhound. Introductions were made with his intended mate and things progressed so well that after just one visit it was announced that he would become a father in about 9 weeks.

With that one question about The O'Brien answered, Cat found herself becoming more curious about The O'Brien's life before her. Perhaps the time had come to try and solve the greatest mystery of all...the mystery of The O'Brien himself.